BATTLE BUGS

THE COBRA CLASH

JACK PATTON

With special thanks to Adrian Bott

Scholastic Children's Books
An imprint of Scholastic Ltd
Euston House, 24 Eversholt Street, London, NW1 1DB, UK
Registered office: Westfield Road, Southam, Warwickshire, CV47 0RA
SCHOLASTIC and associated logos are trademarks and/or
registered trademarks of Scholastic Inc.

First published in the US by Scholastic Inc,. 2015
First published in the UK by Scholastic Ltd, 2016

Text copyright © Hothouse Fiction, 2015
Cover and interior art copyright © Mike Love, 2016
Paper engineering concept © Glen Coleman, 2016

ISBN 978 1407 15793 1

A CIP catalogue record for this book
is available from the British Library.

Printed by CPI Group (UK) Ltd, Croydon, CR0 4YY
Papers used by Scholastic Children's Books are made
from wood grown in sustainable forests.

1 3 5 7 9 10 8 6 4 2

www.scholastic.co.uk

CALL FOR HELP

The students at Burgdale Primary thought their library was pretty cool.

All the computers were new, instead of the sluggish old machines some schools had. You could sit and read by the huge glass windows, or listen to an audiobook in a private cubicle. The librarians were strict, but they weren't as harsh as some could be.

All in all, it was the best place to study if you were in the mood.

Which Max Darwin wasn't.

He'd spread three books out in front of him on his table, but he just couldn't concentrate on them. Steve Bergese and Mike Crabbe sat on either side of him, writing down notes. Mike noticed Max wasn't writing and frowned.

When Max didn't respond, Mike nudged him with an elbow. "Hey, Space Captain Max! You want to come back to Earth, maybe?"

Max blinked. "Sorry. I was daydreaming."

"Probably thinking about *bugs* again," Steve muttered without looking up. "Max has bugs on the brain. I bet centipedes crawl out of his nose when nobody's looking."

Max kicked him under the table, but not too hard, because Steve was the class joker and was like that with everyone.

Besides, he *had* been thinking about bugs: a very special group of bugs, in fact. But he couldn't tell Mike or Steve about them. They'd never believe a word he said.

"Are you boys *talking* over there?" A head wearing dark, round glasses bobbed up over the top of a bookcase, taking them all by surprise. It was Mrs Marquette, the head librarian. The kids of Burgdale all called her Mrs Meerkat, because she had a habit of popping up suddenly, in completely unexpected places.

"No," said Max quickly, shaking his head. Steve and Mike looked down, guiltily.

"Hmph," said Mrs Marquette. She gave the boys a suspicious glare and slowly sank back down again.

Max made a fresh effort to focus on the books in front of him. He had a big history test next period. That was why he, Steve and Mike had met up here. They were *supposed* to be cramming.

But the moment Max tried to read about armies of men shooting arrows at one another or laying siege to castles, he found himself reliving his own memories of Bug Island. Neither Steve nor Mike had ever had to command forces on the battlefield. But Max had.

If only they knew, he thought, and closed his eyes.

Max owned a book that was larger and older than anything in this whole library – his treasured *Encyclopedia of Arthropods*. As well as being a guide to everything you could ever want to know about bugs, it was a magical gateway to another world.

Whenever Max travelled there, he shrunk down to the size of an insect and joined the bug forces in their never-ending battle against the lizards. His bug friends were like boosted versions of bugs from the real world. They were highly intelligent and able to use their real-world abilities in battle.

Bug Island, where they lived, had once been a peaceful paradise. But when an erupting volcano created a bridge of cooled-down lava, the greedy inhabitants of nearby Reptile Island began to cross over and attack. Barton, the titan beetle commander of the Battle Bugs, often called on Max to use his big human brain to help.

Last time Max had visited Bug Island, he'd helped the termite forces build a watch-tower so the bugs could see the lizards coming. It must have done the trick, because Barton hadn't called on him for days now. Max sighed. Maybe the battle was over and the bugs didn't need him any more.

From somewhere among the bags under the table came a sudden *bzzzt*. And again, a longer *bzzzzzzzzt*.

Max's eyes flew open. He glanced up, just in time to see Mrs Meerkat popping up from behind the shelves again.

"Did someone bring a mobile phone to the library?" she asked.

Max, Mike and Steve all looked at one another. "Not us!" each of them said.

"I know a cell phone when I hear one." The librarian scowled. "Just because you've got it set to vibrate doesn't mean you can bring it in here!"

"We're just studying," Max said honestly.

Mrs Meerkat grunted, as if to say *I don't believe a word of it*, but she slunk back

7

behind her desk.

Mike shook his head. "Man. What's her problem?"

"Aren't you going to check your phone?" Max asked.

Mike shrugged. "It's not mine. Mum would never let me bring it to school."

"Me neither," said Steve. "Guess it must be yours, Max."

Puzzled, Max turned back to his books. His phone was in his locker. He'd never have it on him in case it went off in class. *What could have made that noise?* he wondered.

Seconds later, the noise sounded again. This time it was even louder, an urgent-sounding *BZZZT.*

I got it, Max thought. *It's not a mobile*

phone. It's something much more interesting!

Max quickly snatched up his bag from under the table before Mrs Meerkat could come over and start lecturing him again. He needed to get to somewhere quiet and private, fast.

"I'm, uh, just going to find a book," he told his friends. From inside his bag came another *BZZZT*.

A grin spread over Steve's face. "Someone really wants to talk to you, Max. You got a secret admirer?"

"No way!" Max laughed – he knew it was something much better than an admirer.

He turned and headed for the shady end of the library, away from the tall windows.

He ducked behind the stacks and checked to make sure his buddies hadn't followed him so they could listen in. If anyone saw what was about to happen, they wouldn't believe their eyes.

He reached into his backpack and took out the *Encyclopedia of Arthropods*. As he'd expected, the edges of the pages were glowing with a strange silvery light.

BZZZT, went the enormous book. It sounded just like the buzz of a gigantic insect. The cover lifted slightly and the pages fluttered, as if something was struggling to get out.

"I hear you," Max whispered.

He gently opened the book to the pages he'd marked and laid it flat on the floor,

revealing a two-page map of Bug Island. Then he took out the old-fashioned magnifying glass that had come with the encyclopedia and held it over the map.

With a lurch, Max was pulled off his feet. He let out a cry, and then slapped a hand over his mouth quickly. As he went tumbling into the book, shrinking down and down, he heard the shrill voice of Mrs Meerkat demanding, "Who was that? Who made that noise? It's you boys again, isn't it?"

But soon her voice was nothing but a fading echo, and Max was falling down from the sky into the great green mass of Bug Island.

BB

CRASH LANDING

Max could never tell what sort of landing he'd have on Bug Island. Sometimes he landed lightly on leaves or blades of grass, while at other times he might plop down into the sea or even plummet into a pile of rotten plants. He braced himself for the impact, whatever it might be.

Splat!

Mud and water flew up as Max landed feetfirst in a boggy marsh. He sank down to his knees and then, to his relief, bobbed back up again.

"Blurgh," he said aloud to himself, wiping the mud out of his face. He dragged himself out of the slimy hole and up on to the wet ground. "I guess I've had worse landings."

Max looked around, wondering where on Bug Island he was. The sun was just coming up, and the gnarled trees all around him cast long shadows over the wet ground. Long vines hung down from the branches, and pools of water shone bright as scattered coins in the early sunlight. Here and there, strange plants and flowers sprouted from the marsh. Their blues, reds and yellows blazed against the murky brown background of the swamp. Max recognized the gaping jaws of a Venus flytrap and shuddered. Hopefully his bug friends knew to stay well away from *that* plant!

There were no bugs on the ground for him to warn, but from overhead came a constant whirr and whiz, as if airplanes were flying past. Max looked up to see an amazing stream of flying bugs hurtling by.

Dragonflies droned above, their bodies gleaming like jewels and their bulbous heads as shiny as armoured helmets. Other, even bigger bugs zoomed past, too. Max stood like a pedestrian beside a busy turnpike watching them go by: damselflies, May bugs and huge dark bugs he'd never even seen before.

"What's going on?" he muttered. So many bugs all rushing the same way wasn't normal. Something big was happening on Bug Island. Maybe Barton had called for a mass attack, or maybe the bugs were going to battle, to finish the lizards once and for all.

"Hey! Where are you all going?" he yelled. "It's me, Max!"

None of the flying bugs looked his way, and not one of them even slowed down.

Max clambered across a slushy, squishy swamp and stood gasping on a bank of moss. He jumped up and down, waving his arms and yelling, "Over here!"

One of the dragonflies zoomed low, and for a moment Max thought it was going to stop for him. No such luck. It rocketed past, its legs brushing his head.

"Can't stop!" it droned. "This is an emergency. Code red! Code red!"

The next second it vanished from sight, plunging in amongst the jungle trees with all the other flying bugs.

"Uh-oh." Max said. "That doesn't sound good."

Without knowing where he was, he had no idea how he was supposed to help. But at least the flying bugs seemed to know where they were going – if they were heading westward, then that's where he would have to go, too.

Max set off at a run, following the dragon-flies. His trainers, still sodden with muddy water, squelched loudly as he ran. Every few seconds he glanced up to make sure he was still going the right way, dodging trees and fallen branches as he went. As he ducked a fat, spiky vine, he glanced up again, but this time his foot gave way beneath him in the wet ground. With nothing to grab on to but the razor-sharp shrub, he stumbled to the ground.

"Argh," he yelled, as he plunged into a boggy pool. Thick, oily bubbles rose and burst around him. "Gross. Can this day get any worse?"

He wrenched himself upward, trying to pull himself out of the gooey mess. But for some reason, the more he kicked and floundered, the deeper he sank.

"What the—" Max began. Soon he was up to his waist. Apparently this day was about to get *a lot* worse.

With a jolt he realized what it was: "Quicksand!" Every time he moved he was getting more and more stuck, and sinking all the while. If he didn't get out, he'd be sucked under for ever.

Max peered around, frantically. Luckily, there was a root protruding from the mud just ahead of him. It would only have been the size of a hair to full-sized Max, but to the bug-sized version it was thick as a rope. Leaning forward in the slurping mess of bog, he reached out until his fingertips ached. He just managed to wrap his hands around it and pulled as hard as he could. He leaned forward, using the root to pull himself to the edge of the bog once more, when the root broke free in his hands with a loud tearing noise.

"Nooo!" Max cried. Now he really started to panic. A deep gurgle from below told him he was sinking fast. His only hope was that one of the flying bugs would hear his cries for help.

"Stuck human being here!" he yelled at the top of his voice. "Help!"

The dragonflies just shot by, one after the other. Either they couldn't hear him or they thought their emergency was more important.

That's when Max had an idea. He waved the broken root in the air towards the low-flying bugs. Swooshing with all his strength, he just managed to clip the underside of one of the fast-moving creatures.

"Gotcha!" he cried.

This time, the giant black shape broke formation and came hurtling down towards him. It swept past overhead, giving Max a glimpse of its airplane-sized body and splayed legs, before landing opposite him on the bank with an earthshaking thump.

Now that he could see it clearly, Max gaped in awe. The insect had two colossal mandibles jutting from its head, like an earwig's pincers but at least twice the size. Its two giant sets of wings were far larger than its body.

I recognize that, Max thought. *It's a giant dobsonfly – the biggest aquatic flying insect in the world.*

"WHAT'S GOING ON?" boomed the giant dobsonfly. "ARE YOU TRYING TO MAKE ME CRASH-LAND?"

"No!" Max explained his situation quickly, feeling the quicksand rise to his chest. "I need help getting out of here!"

"OH, I SEE. THEN WHY DIDN'T YOU JUST SAY SO?"

I did try, Max thought, as the dobsonfly hovered over him.

Max kept very still as the dobsonfly slowly closed his pincers around his body.

One slip, and those sharp, curved mandibles might skewer him. But the giant insect was surprisingly gentle as he carefully hauled Max out of the bubbling, gurgling sand.

"Thanks!" Max gasped, safe on the solid ground again. "Those things really come in handy!"

"WELL, I'M A LIFTER AND HAULER, YOU SEE—"

Max winced and covered his ears. "Could you maybe talk more quietly? I'm gonna go deaf!"

"Sorry about that," the dobsonfly said. "You've got to shout to be heard with all those dragonflies droning up above."

Max knew about that all too well.

"I'm Dobs, the logistics bug. I transport all kinds of things across the island to help with the war effort."

"I'm Max," he said. "What's all the commotion about?"

"They haven't told us yet. There's some sort of emergency in the bug camp. Wait – did you say Max? You're General Barton's special adviser, aren't you? The human being!"

"That's me." Max grinned.

"Then you need to get to Barton right away. Need a lift?"

Max clambered gratefully on to Dobs's back and they took off in a roar of wings.

After a short flight through the trees, they touched down in a clearing full of feverish activity. Bugs were racing back and forth all around. Fireflies blinked frantic messages to one another. Max heard fly scouts delivering their reports:

"Nothing new."

"No sightings."

"Not even a trail to follow."

Max barely had a chance to get off Dobs's back before he saw a familiar shape pushing through the hordes of busy bugs, its carapace large as an overturned boat, its mandibles like antlers. It was Barton, the titan beetle, commander of the Battle Bug forces.

"Out of the way!" Barton ordered. The smaller bugs quickly scurried out of his path.

Barton was always serious, but never

this stern and grave. "What's going on, General?" Max asked.

"Max, it's a disaster. The lizards mounted a surprise attack last night."

"Oh, no!" Max gasped. "Was it bad? Were many bugs hurt?"

"It's even worse than that," Barton said gravely. "They captured one of our best offi- cers. It's Spike – he's been bugnapped!"

BUGNAPPED!

"Spike," Max said, hardly able to believe it – the emperor scorpion was his best friend on Bug Island. "But he's so tough! Those claws, and that sting . . . How could any lizard take him down?"

"They caught us off-guard," Barton explained, clearly miserable. "And what's more, it was an air strike. The lizards have never tried anything of the kind before."

"But lizards can't fly," Max cried. Being able to fly had always been one of the bugs' biggest tactical advantages. Although the lizards had allied with a group of greedy birds once, the lizards themselves would always be stuck on the ground.

"They used gliding lizards. They waited until the middle of the night to do it, too. Do you know how much noise a gliding lizard makes in flight?"

"None at all?" Max guessed.

"Exactly. They swooped in from all directions at once, so our bugs didn't even have an escape route."

"Clever," Max said sourly.

Barton nodded. "Komodo planned this one well, I'll give him that."

Max wished he could have been here on Bug Island the night before. Together, he and Spike were an unstoppable team. They never could have bugnapped the scorpion if he'd been there.

"General, what exactly happened to him? Was he hurt?"

"The lizards bundled Spike away before the bugs could do anything to stop them. He put up a fight, although I don't think he was hurt."

Max felt a little better. However, the lizards were obviously keeping Spike alive for some reason – but why?

"I've got all my best bugs on the job,"

Barton said. "The lizards won't get away with this!"

Suddenly, right on cue, a flickering orange light high up in the trees caught Max's eye: a firefly signal! The next moment, an old friend of his flew down, bustling through the bugs in the clearing and coming to a halt right in front of them.

"Glower!"

"Good to see you again, Max," he said. The firefly was head of the underground bug resistance, tasked with picking up intelligence from across the island and making sure it got back to central command. "It's a shame we have to meet like this, but one of our agents picked up some news on Spike."

"What is it?" Barton barked. "There's no time to lose."

"We've received a personal message from Komodo," Glower said.

Max was shocked. The giant komodo dragon lizard was the head of the reptile forces. He never stooped to the level of actually sending messages to the bugs. This must have been serious.

"What did he say?" Max demanded.

"My agent remembered it word for word . . ." Glower began. "He said, 'We are holding the scorpion known as Spike. He is currently unharmed, but he is being held at the volcano on Reptile Island. There is no hope of rescue. We therefore present you with a choice: Give up the fight by sundown and surrender Bug Island to us, or Spike will be thrown into the burning lava.'"

Glower stopped. Max and the bugs looked at one another in shock. A frightened silence settled over the camp. Barton's long head slowly drooped in what might have been sorrow, or pain. "So he wants us to give up our friend or give up our island," he said, eventually. Barton faced an impossible choice, and they all knew it.

"It's simple," Max said firmly. "We do neither. Instead, *we go and get Spike back*."

Buzzes and clicks of agreement swept through the bug ranks.

"But how?" Glower asked. "No bug has ever set so much as an antenna on Reptile Island!"

"What's your thinking?" Barton asked Max. "There's no way we can go on an all-out attack in unknown terrain."

"Why not?" a nearby mantis asked. "We could storm the place. Take the fight to them!" He scissored his sharp foreclaws in anticipation.

"No. Barton's right," Max said firmly. "If we mounted a full attack, they'd see us coming from a mile away, and Spike would be toast."

"So what *can* we do?" Glower asked.

"We use *stealth*," he replied, thinking back to all those sneaky moves the armies had used in his history lessons. "We'll get a small team together and do the unthinkable. We cross over to Reptile Island!"

"What?" Glower said. "That's impossible. It's never been done before!"

Murmuring broke out all around.

"Small team?"

"The human's braver than he looks, isn't he?"

Barton considered Max's idea carefully before answering. "A stealth raid into reptile territory?" His antennae twitched in concentration. "It might be our only hope of getting Spike back . . ."

"What do you think?" Max asked.

"We'll do it," declared Barton, finally. "It's time to put together a SWAT team."

"Yes!" Max cried. "Let's go get Spike!"

The bugs in the clearing let out a cheer.

"Although, a bug SWAT team?" Max

laughed. "This is the first time I've ever heard of bugs wanting to be swatted!"

The bugs all looked at him blankly.

"Forget it," Max said. "Just a little human-being humour!"

Barton explained what a SWAT team was, bug-style. It stood for Stingers, Webs And Toxins, and you needed at least one sting-ing insect, one web spinner and one who could poison enemies.

"I nominate Buzz for stinger and Webster for web-spinner," Max suggested.

Buzz, the hornet captain of the flying bugs, and Webster, the trapdoor spider, both stepped forward.

"I'd be honoured to accept!" said Buzz.

"Muh . . . m-m-me, too," stammered Webster.

"You and I are team leaders," Barton told Max. "Which just leaves us with one space to fill. I think I know who our poison specialist should be."

"I accept!" called a deep voice.

Max turned around to see a large shape gliding towards them on a hundred legs, trampling smaller bugs underfoot and ignoring their buzzes of protest. It was a giant centipede, the largest one Max had ever seen, gleaming and black.

"Max, this is my newest warrior. Meet Gigantus."

Gigantus reared up, waving her front legs and showing off a pair of curved fang-like forcipules. "You want venom? I got venom!"

Barton chuckled. "Gigantus has been looking forward to a good fight for some time. Isn't that right?"

"Sir yes sir!" she barked.

Webster cowered away from the giant centipede. "I hope she scares the lizards," the spider whispered to Max, "because she scares the daylights out of me. Look at her: armour plating all over, dozens of legs that can climb over just about anything, powerful jaws, and venom, too. She's unstoppable."

Max gave Webster a comforting pat. "Just try to remember she's on our side. OK, SWAT team, let's get moving—"

"I VOLUNTEER FOR THE SWAT TEAM, TOO!" boomed Dobs.

Max and Barton glanced at each other. "Go on . . ." Max said.

"I can scout from the air, and I can lift huge loads. What if Spike's behind a boulder, or something? I could move it. And these jaws of mine are strong! I could give a lizard a nip he wouldn't forget!"

"I'm sorry, Dobs," Barton said. "I know you're brave, but you're not really a fighting bug."

"I could be."

Max sighed. "The thing is, Dobs, the whole point of this team is to be stealthy, and, well . . . you're huge. They'd see you coming from a mile away."

"I suppose so," Dobs said gloomily. "I understand. Sorry. I just wanted to help."

"Well, that was awkward," muttered Buzz, once Dobs was out of earshot. Max felt bad for the big insect who'd pulled him out of the quicksand. He just wanted to help.

The bugs took a moment to make sure they were in top fighting condition. Buzz groomed her wings, Webster checked his spinnerets, and Gigantus flexed her poison injectors to make sure they were ready. A gleaming drop of venom dripped down from the tip of one and lay at Max's feet like a deadly jewel.

"I wouldn't touch that if I were you," the centipede said.

"I wasn't planning on it," Max replied.

At Barton's signal, the SWAT team trooped down to the beach. Churning waves crashed against the lava bridge, flooding the grey-black rocks with foaming water. There, at the far end of the bridge, stood Reptile Island and the looming volcano.

"Ever since we were grubs, the shadow of Reptile Island has fallen over us all," Barton said. "Today, we make bug history. We will be the first bugs ever to travel there, deep into the enemy homeland itself!"

Max looked up at the volcano's distant slopes. Somewhere in there, Spike was being held prisoner.

"Ready?" Barton asked them.

Max nodded. "Let's do this!"

BB

SWAT

The sun was just above the horizon, casting a glittering carpet of light across the sea. The world seemed peaceful, but Max knew that feeling wouldn't last.

The lava bridge lay before them, a solidified flow of molten rock. It reminded Max of the puddled mess that wax crayons make when you leave them in the hot sun.

It wasn't much of a bridge at all, Max thought to himself. It was nothing but a mass of cooled lava stretching across the sea between the two islands. Bridges that were built on purpose had guardrails and supports. This one was nothing but a soaking wet tightrope in comparison.

"Want me to go first?" Gigantus offered.

Max shook his head. He thought of Spike, miserable and alone in the lizards' prison, and the thought gave him courage. He stepped out on to the rocks.

At first, it wasn't so bad. The humps and ripples of cooled lava were easy to walk across, and although the waves sprayed cold water all over Max, he didn't let it slow him down. In fact, it was washing off some of the muck from the swamp, which suited Max fine.

Barton opened his wing cases and flew up into the air, with Buzz close behind. "We'll scout ahead and meet you on the other side!" Buzz shouted down to them.

"Good luck!" Max waved as they shot off into the distance.

Webster and Gigantus crawled along behind Max, keeping close to the middle of the bridge so the waves wouldn't wash them off. Max dropped to all fours to clamber across the wet rocks. That way, if he slipped, he wouldn't tumble into the water.

The further they went, the more slippery and treacherous the rocks became. Max thought of calling Barton and Buzz back to airlift them out of there, but the two flying bugs were well out of sight.

The next second, his foot skidded on a patch of slimy green seaweed left behind by the tide. He fell with a shout of surprise, and only just managed to keep from rolling over the edge. "That was too close!"

"A-are you OK, Max?" Webster whispered.

"There's nothing to hold on to," Max said. "These rocks are too slippery. See how the lava slopes up at the far end? We'll never get up there."

"We could edge around the outside where the slope's gentler," Webster suggested.

"Not if these waves get any rougher. We'll be washed over the side." Max wished he'd had time to get the termites to build him a raft, or something. Or the hornets could have flown them across. But no – the lizards would see them coming, and Spike would be finished. There *had* to be a way.

Max looked over his shoulder in search of Gigantus, expecting to see the impressive centipede warrior climbing over the rocks with ease. But Gigantus was in trouble, too. Her fifty pairs of legs couldn't get much of a grip on the oozing rocks, and she stop-started towards them like a truck stuck in a muddy field.

Max felt a tickle on his back and realized Webster was tapping him lightly with one of his legs. "Um, Max, I might have an idea . . . that is . . . if you're not too busy . . ."

"Let's hear it. Right now I'll consider anything."

"What if I go on ahead and make you both a nice sticky web line to hang on to? That way you and Gigantus will be safe."

Max had to admit it was a good plan. "But what about you?"

"Don't worry about me. I'm a spider. I'm good at climbing," Webster said, trembling slightly.

Max smiled to see his shy friend being so brave. "Lead the way!"

Webster scuttled off across the lava bridge. As he moved, the spinnerets at the back of his body wiggled and a long line of silk emerged. It gleamed like a metal cable, but Max knew it was stronger than steel. Spider silk was a miracle material, super-strong, and flexible, too. Scientists back in the human world would love to unlock all its secrets if they could.

Max grabbed hold of it. Miracle material or not, it felt gluey and a little gross. Still, having something to hang on to was better than being washed out to sea.

With Gigantus close behind, he steadily worked his way across the rocks. The centipede clung to Webster's web line as the wind and the waves buffeted her.

"I don't really need this web line, you know," Gigantus shouted, "but it would hurt Webster's feelings if I didn't use it."

Max rolled his eyes. "Sure."

Steadily, carefully, Max inched his way across the lava bridge. The wind was whipping the sea up so much that the bridge behind him was awash with foaming seawater. *Unless this weather calms down*, he thought, *there'll be no way back.*

Up ahead, where the lava bridge formed a ramp up the beach, he saw Barton and Buzz circling in the air. Webster led the way to a rock platform jutting out of the side of the bridge, above the waves. From there, they could see Reptile Island up close for the first time. A harsh landscape of rolling sand dunes and jagged rocks stretched before them, with only a few patches of scrub to break the desolation. The whole place looked mean, sinister and completely without mercy, like the lizards who lived there. "We made it." Max said, wringing the seawater out of his sleeve. "So far, so good."

"A little *too* good, if you ask me," Barton said. "Neither Buzz nor I have seen a single lizard yet. Where are they?"

Max looked across the beach. Nothing moved on the sand dunes or the rocks, and the slopes of the volcano were empty. It was eerily quiet.

"Maybe they're not up yet," Webster said. "Reptiles are cold-blooded, so they can be slow to get started in the morning."

"Let's fly up and down the beach and do reconnaissance," suggested Buzz.

"No!" Max said. "They might spot you. Let's stay close to the ground, but try to get a better look. That rock down there looks good."

The bugs scrambled down the side of the lava bridge, across the beach sand, and up on to the rock Max had pointed out. He looked from horizon to horizon, but it seemed as if all of Reptile Island had been abandoned. Not even so much as a tail-tip showed.

"Something doesn't seem right..." Max said.

Suddenly, beneath Max's feet, the rock lurched. "Whoa... what's going on?" The rock rose slowly up, toppling him on to his back.

"The beach is collapsing!" wailed Webster.

"No it's not," growled Gigantus. "The rock's moving by itself!"

All the bugs clung on tight to the rock as it rose up again. Max peered over the edge and found he was looking down at the top of a head – a mean-eyed, wrinkly head with a snapping beak. When Max saw the thing's leathery flippers, he knew what they were really standing on.

"Uh-oh. This is no rock. It's a giant turtle!"

"Look!" Webster squealed.

All across the beach, other humped forms were heaving themselves up out of the sand. Heads swayed from side to side.

Beaks clacked and snapped.

Max gulped. There wasn't just one turtle. There were dozens. And they all looked very, very hungry.

BB

TERRIBLE TURTLES

The giant turtle leaned to one side, then the other, hissing in fury. Max and the bugs struggled to hold on as they were thrown wildly around.

"It's trying to buck us off!" roared Gigantus.

Max knew what would happen if it succeeded. A loggerhead turtle's jaws were strong enough to crunch through crab shell. Even Gigantus's armour would be no use against the turtle. The stunned bugs would be gobbled up in seconds.

"Barton, Buzz, take off and try to distract them. Webster, Gigantus, you're with me. Run for that rocky outcrop as fast as you can." Max pointed at a raised mass of rock that rose out of the sand like a craggy cliff.

Barton and Buzz zoomed in front of the turtle and swarmed around its mean face and snapping beak. "Hey!" Buzz taunted. "Think you can get me, you lumbering lump of mud?"

"Just watch me!" the turtle bellowed. It lunged at her, snapping furiously at the empty air. The nimble hornet dodged easily out of the way and hovered, making a very rude-sounding *bzzzzt*.

"Quick, while Buzz has his attention," Max told Webster and Gigantus. He pushed himself down the glossy, bumpy slope of the turtle's shell, slid for some distance, and fell down on to the sand.

Max set off at a run, heading for the rocky outcrop. Gigantus and Webster scurried along beside him.

All across the beach, the other turtles moved to intercept them. They were slow, dragging themselves along with their flippers, but there were so many of them that Max had to zigzag and double back on himself to stay out of their way.

His luck had to run out soon – and it did.

Just as it seemed like they had a clear path to the rocks, a turtle burst up from the sand right in front of them. Gigantus and Webster escaped to the left and right, but Max struggled to stop in time and fell head over heels.

"Oh, how nice!" leered the turtle. "I've only just woken up, and breakfast's already here!"

Max struggled to get up. The turtle laughed at his efforts and snapped at him. Only a quick roll to the side saved Max's skin.

"Stay still so I can eat you," the turtle groused.

"Not a chance," said Max.

Once again, he struggled to get to his

feet. The turtle lurched forward to snap him in two, but then, out of nowhere, a glistening spray of webbing plastered its eyes like sticky string from a can.

"Argh!" it roared, trying to scrape its face clean with its clumsy flippers, and failing. "What is this stuff?"

"It's webbing, you big bully," said Webster.

"Webster!" Max yelled, seeing the spider crouching beside him. "You came back for me!"

"I couldn't leave you behind," said the spider. "But now I think we'd better run."

"Where's Gigantus?"

"She's at the rocks already."

"Great. Too bad she couldn't stick around and help!"

Max got ready to make the final dash, but the turtles were closing in. There was nowhere to go.

But there was one way, he thought, if he was brave enough to take it. "Come on!" he yelled, running straight towards the turtle's snapping jaws. Twisting and jerking right at the last minute, Max and Webster dived under the turtle's screeching head, scrambled between its flippers, and darted right under its mottled body.

"Where'd my breakfast go?" howled the turtle.

"Guess you'll have to go hungry," Max muttered. He pulled himself across the sand under the turtle's body, until he could see clear daylight at the other side. As he scrambled to his feet, the turtle lashed out with a flurry of bites, but instead of gobbling up Max, he bit one of his fellow turtles on the nose. Soon, the aggressive turtles were fighting among themselves.

Max and Webster dashed the rest of the way across to the outcrop. Gigantus was dangling from the top, holding on with only a couple of her legs. "Come on up!" she shouted. "Quick, before those turtles figure out where you went."

Max felt sorry for doubting Gigantus, now that he saw she was waiting there to help them. While Webster scuttled quickly up the steep side of the rocks, Max ran, jumped, and grabbed hold of Gigantus's body.

"Hold on tight," grunted the centipede. Gigantus began to heave her long body up and over the ledge, taking Max with her. Down below on the beach, the turtles had stopped fighting for long enough to figure out where the bugs had gone. They shuffled up to the foot of the outcrop, yelling and jeering, calling for the tasty bugs to come back.

Gigantus hauled Max up to the safety of the ledge. A quick look down confirmed it: The turtles were marooned on the beach, unable to follow them up the craggy rocks.

"Get back here, you—" they started, but Max and the bugs didn't stick around to find out what the turtles had in store.

Buzz and Barton landed next to them, and together the SWAT team looked out across the landscape further inland, wondering what deadly dangers still lay in wait.

The volcano loomed up in front of them. A never-ending plume of black smoke rose from its crater. Down the side trickled a steady stream of lava, lighting up the sandy ground with fierce reddish-orange light.

"What now?" Gigantus rasped.

"We know Spike's up there somewhere, so that's where we have to go," Max said. "Barton and Buzz had better scout ahead again. The rest of us can make our way up to the volcano's side. We all need to keep our eyes open and see if we can spot the cave where they're keeping Spike."

"Roger!" Buzz flew up and away, with Barton close behind. Max, Gigantus and Webster cautiously made their way across the rocky ground. Max noticed deep cracks here and there, which would be all too easy to fall into.

"Max?" whispered Webster. "I'm worried about something."

Nothing new there, Max thought. "What's on your mind?" he asked the spider.

"What if those turtles go and warn General Komodo that we're here?"

Webster had a point. Max mulled it over. "Lucky for us, they're not very bright. But one of them is bound to think of warning Komodo sooner or later. They can't move fast, though. We've still got a head start at least."

A deep rumble came from the volcano. Beneath their feet the earth trembled.

Webster shuddered and drew his legs in. "Was that . . . what I think it was?"

"Probably," said Max. "That volcano's still active. No time to lose. Let's go!"

But to Max's dismay, they only made it a short distance before yet another disaster struck. The earth rumbled and a wide crack opened in the ground out in front of them. For Max and the bugs, it was like a canyon in the middle of the desert, flooded with flowing lava. The red-hot molten rock gurgled and spurted like a living thing as it slid sluggishly by below them. Waves of heat made Max's mouth feel dry and his eyes sore. If he got any closer he'd be burned to a crisp.

"Maybe we can find another way around," he started to say, but Gigantus was already surging forward on her many legs.

"Leave it to me!" the centipede cried.

Gigantus stretched herself out like a makeshift army bridge, grabbing on to the far side and spanning the gap with her body. The sight reminded Max of soldiers forming a human bridge to help stranded people across a river.

"You go first," Max told Webster. He didn't want the spider left fretting on the chasm's edge.

Webster obediently scampered out across Gigantus's body. Max held his breath. Luckily, the spider made it all the way. His eight legs spread out across Gigantus's back helped him keep his balance.

"Come on, Max!" Gigantus grunted. "I'm being roasted here!"

Moving on all fours, Max climbed on to Gigantus's segmented back. The centipede's body sagged alarmingly as it took his weight. He scrambled along Gigantus's length as quickly as he could, trying not to look down into the lava.

The volcano rumbled again, much louder this time, and the earth shook. Suddenly, Gigantus's back legs lost their grip on the rocky ground. The centipede scrabbled madly at thin air as her whole body swung down – Max slammed into the wall of the chasm.

"Argh!" he yelled as he bounced off the rocky wall. He reached out frantically for something to grab on to, but could only find thin air . . .

BB

HIDDEN ENEMY

With a desperate lunge, Max reached out for anything he could get his hands on. In an instant he grabbed at one of Gigantus's many legs and the centipede yelled in surprise.

Below his swaying feet, the lava bubbled and spat. A stench of scorched rubber wafted up. The soles of his trainers were starting to melt!

"Gigantus, help me!" Max yelled, breathlessly.

"I'm trying," bellowed Gigantus. She scrabbled with all her lower legs at once, but only a few of them came anywhere near the wall. Instead of grabbing on, they just brushed it.

Max knew his weight was dragging the centipede into the chasm. There was only one thing to do. He had to get off Gigantus's back before they both fell into the lava.

Using Gigantus's legs like a ladder, Max began to climb. The giant centipede howled as Max clambered up. "That hurts!"

"Sorry! It's our only chance!"

One by one, Max took hold of the thick black legs and pulled himself up. As the chasm wall began to give way and Gigantus slipped slowly down towards the molten lava river, Max scrambled up and out over the ledge.

Then, he and Webster both grabbed hold of one of Gigantus's front legs each. Together they pulled the giant centipede out of the crevasse until enough of her legs were on the flat ground for her to climb the rest of the way.

"Thanks," the centipede said, sounding gruff and tough again. "You two are stronger than you look."

Max brushed himself down, but there was no time to relax – not while Spike was still trapped somewhere on Reptile Island. The trio pressed on towards the mountainside.

Two distant specks burst out of the shroud of smoke and came hurtling at them. Max squinted, trying to see if they were flying lizards. To his relief, it was only Barton and Buzz, back from their scouting mission.

"Did you find where he's being held?" Max called.

"We did better than that," Buzz said, sweeping in low to land. "We've found Spike."

"Yes!" Max punched the air. "Is he OK?"

"He's alive," Barton said, "but he's hurt his leg. He's been poisoned, by the look of it.

He can't climb out on his own. We'll need to help him."

A suspicious thought crossed Max's mind. "Did you see any lizards?"

"None. They may be out on patrol. Or they may be so confident of our surrender that they didn't bother to guard Spike."

I doubt that, Max thought darkly. The lizards knew how important Spike was, and how dangerous. There was bound to be a guard here somewhere, even if they couldn't see it yet.

Buzz and Barton led the way up the side of the rocky volcano. Max felt uneasy, as if he were being watched. There was a reptile of *some* kind nearby. He'd bet his life on it. But what sort of beast would be powerful enough to guard Spike, the emperor scorpion?

Barton landed next to Max and pointed out a pitlike crevasse up ahead. It looked like it had been scraped out of the mountainside by titanic hands. "There it is."

"Everyone stay close and keep quiet," Max warned.

All Max's senses were on high alert as he crept up to the edge of the pit. Nothing moved or made a sound, but the feeling of being watched was stronger than ever. Although this was the perfect chance to scout out Reptile Island and get valuable intel on the enemy, he made up his mind then and there to get Spike out and get away fast. This place gave him the creeps.

He looked down and saw Spike far down in the shadows, waving his pincers happily. "Max! You came to get me!"

"We wouldn't leave you behind, buddy. We even brought a SWAT team!"

Spike saluted briskly when he saw Barton. "Sorry I got caught, sir. Those filthy lizards knocked me out! Next thing I knew, I woke up here." He waved his injured leg. "I'd climb out, but one of them bit me."

Webster shuffled forward. "K-keep still. I'll drop a web line and we can winch you up with it."

"Hurry up!" Spike scuttled back and forth eagerly. "That guard will be back any minute."

"Guard?" Max gasped. "You didn't mention a guard!"

Suddenly, an ominous shadow loomed over Max.

"And what is thisss?"

The bugs turned quickly at the sound of the strange hissing voice that was edging ever closer.

What Max saw then would haunt his nightmares. Spike's guard was an Indian cobra, hooded and fanged, many times larger than the bugs. Cobras were frightening enough when they were normal size, but this gigantic creature was a true monster.

"Er . . ." Max tried to stammer a reply, but was frozen to the ground in fright.

Suddenly, Barton leapt into action. "I'll

hold him off," he growled. "You get Spike."

"Wait!" Max yelled. "It's venomous – be careful!" But the brave general was already flying into action.

Startled, the cobra reared up as it saw Barton coming. "*Sssilly* bug! You are really trying to fight *me*?"

Barton's response was to hurl himself at the cobra like a buzzing meteor and latch on to its upper body with his strong mandibles. Max knew those pincers were strong as a vice, and the cobra had underestimated Barton badly, but they were still in a lot of trouble.

"Buzz, fly back to Bug Island as fast as you can. We need some serious reinforcements."

"Roger that, Max!"

The cobra thrashed its body to and fro, trying to shake Barton loose. With one determined fling, it threw him backwards on to the sand. The bug general lay with his legs kicking in the air, helpless, and for a second Max feared the worst. Then Barton righted himself again and flew back into the fight. "Not finished yet," he muttered.

"Quick, Webster, get that web line down!" Max said.

Webster shot a glistening web rope into the pit, which Spike caught and wound around his pincer. "Haul away!" he shouted.

Webster began to tug, helping Spike to scramble out of the pit. He was halfway up when Max heard a strange, frantic buzzing sound. The cobra had the advantage on Barton. It lunged again and again, trying to strike the commander with its venomous fangs.

"Barton's not strong enough to beat it on his own," Gigantus said.

"Hurry, Webster! We need Spike in this fight!"

But though Webster was pulling for all he was worth, Spike wasn't out of the pit yet.

And the cobra was slithering straight at them . . .

SURROUNDED!

Gigantus slid forward on her hundred legs and formed a living barrier, blocking Max and Webster from the approaching cobra. "You two pull Spike out, and leave the reptile to me!"

Max grabbed Webster's sticky silk rope and helped the spider haul Spike out of the crevasse. Spike managed to hook one pincer over the edge.

The cobra's hooded shadow fell over them all. It hissed a challenge to Gigantus: "Wretched little crawler. Grovelling bug. Who are you to *s-s-stand againssst* me?"

Gigantus struck like a whiplash. Quicker than any of them could have expected, she rushed at the snake and clamped her poison injectors together, trying to bite. Startled, the cobra recoiled.

"You talk a lot," growled Gigantus, "but I'm going to bring you down to size."

The cobra went on the attack, striking, and striking again, but Gigantus dodged smoothly out of the way both times. Her segmented body could loop and coil like a ribbon streamer, and it drove the cobra crazy. The cobra struck for a third time. Gigantus darted out of the way, and the cobra's head whacked against a stone half-buried in the sand.

"That hurt," the cobra hissed, with murderous anger in its voice. It swayed dizzily, looking around to see where Gigantus had gone.

"Really? Well, this is going to hurt a lot more," Gigantus said.

Before the stunned cobra could react, the centipede had rushed up its long body. Like a vampire, Gigantus plunged her venomous barbs into the snake's throat.

The poison went into action instantly. The cobra's mouth yawned wide and it twitched along its entire length. Then, all at once, the cobra flopped down in the dust like a loose heap of old rope.

Meanwhile, Spike had scrambled over the edge of the pit. "Nice!" he told Gigantus. "Did you kill it?"

"My venom's not deadly," Gigantus admitted. "But the reptile's paralysed. Right now he can't move, but he'll recover soon."

Max wondered what to do about the fallen cobra. "Let's roll it down into the pit. Otherwise it might come after us."

Together, he and the bugs bundled the hapless snake down into the crevasse. It glared at them with eyes full of hate. Spike gave it the final push. "Bye!" he yelled as it tumbled down into the dark. "That's for biting my leg!"

Max glanced up at the sky, wondering when Buzz was coming back. The cobra might be defeated, but they had a long way to go before they were out of danger.

"Spike, can you walk?" he asked.

"Just about," Spike said. "I, um, can't carry you yet, though. Sorry."

"No problem. Let's just get you out of here."

Together, Max and the bugs edged their way back down the side of the volcano. It was slow going with poor Spike hobbling along, and to make things worse, the volcano kept making rumbling noises.

"It's still bubbling away," Webster squeaked.

Max hoped the spider was just fretting.

But then a roar sounded behind them, and a fresh wave of lava came flooding over the very top of the crater like milk boiling over on a stove. It gushed down the volcano's side in a thick, glowing tide. It wasn't as powerful as the eruption that had created the land bridge, but it was still spewing out enough lava to cause the bugs trouble.

"Great!" Spike cried. "That's all we need!"

"Can this get any worse?" Gigantus grunted.

Webster's voice was a trembling, tiny peep: "Yes, it can. Look!"

The cobra's head rose out of the prison pit. Still groggy from Gigantus's poison, it slithered down the slope in their direction.

"Get back here!" it hissed at them.

Everyone put on a fresh burst of speed, including Spike, though it hurt him to do so. With Gigantus acting as a bridge, they crossed from rock to rock, staying out of the way of the pools of lava that had already begun to form.

Soon, they were almost halfway back down the volcano. Max could see the beach in the distance. There was no sign of the turtles, and the seas had calmed down. The lava bridge looked like it would be easy to cross.

He glanced behind and saw the wave of lava still surging down the mountain, but not fast enough to reach them. The cobra was nowhere in sight.

"I think our luck's finally changed," he told his bug friends.

"It has indeed," said a gloating, raspy voice. "In fact, I'd say your luck has RUN OUT!"

"That voice," Barton said. "That's . . ."

A gigantic reptilian head loomed up over the ledge. General Komodo himself slithered into view, heaving his massive body up and into their path. There was no way to reach the lava bridge now.

"It's Komodo. Get back!" Max yelled. "Find another way down."

But the words died in his throat as he saw what was coming. From all sides, greenish winged lizards were swooping down on them.

"Gliding lizards, *again*," roared Spike. "I hate those sneaky things!"

The lizards flopped down to land in perfect formation, surrounding the group completely.

All the SWAT team could do was huddle together, brandishing their stings, mandibles or fists, as the lizards advanced. Steadily they closed in, leaving no gap to escape through. Komodo loomed over them all, a ghastly grin of victory on his face.

"This is the moment I have long been waiting for," he said with relish. "Today, General Barton and his human friend Max will die. And Bug Island will be ours!"

Max could see no way to escape this time. The lizards had them surrounded. The battle for Bug Island was finally over . . . but his side had lost.

"Did you really think Reptile Island would be so easy to enter?" Komodo mocked. "This has all been a trap. And you blundered right into it!"

GREAT REPTILICUS

"Battle Bugs," said General Barton, "this could be our last stand. Fight like you've never fought before."

"Don't be a fool," General Komodo spat. "You're surrounded and outnumbered."

"Maybe we should listen to what Komodo has to say?" Max suggested, giving Barton a meaningful glance. He hoped the bug general understood what he was thinking. *Komodo loves to give long speeches, so maybe while he's gloating at us, we'll be able to think of a way out of this.*

"I say we fight!" Gigantus roared. "Let's take some lizards down with us."

"Stand down, Gigantus. We'll do as Max says," Barton said.

Komodo chuckled. "The human being always was the brains of your pathetic operation, Barton. Which is why I waited until he was off the island before putting my plan into action."

"Plan?" Max blinked. "What plan?"

Now Komodo roared with laughter. His gliding lizard minions joined in, mocking and pointing at the bugs.

"What's so funny?" Spike shouted. For some reason, that just made them laugh all the more.

"Do you really think I happened to be here by chance, when I have the whole of Reptile Island to roam around?"

Max understood. "I get it. You *knew* we'd be here, didn't you?"

"Naturally. I knew you bugs would rush to the rescue of your friend and comrade in arms. Especially you, human."

Spike moaned as the truth dawned on him, too. "I was bait in your trap!" he yelled.

"Why else would we capture you?" Komodo gloated. "It's not as if you were important."

Spike scuttled around inside the ring

of lizards, waving his pincers in the air and shouting with fury. A gliding lizard nipped at Spike, taunting him. The scorpion rushed forward to attack, but Webster stopped him.

"Leave it, S-Spike."

"You bugs are so predictable," Komodo hissed, flicking his tongue in and out. "Now you're trapped, and there's no way out. And no hope for the rest of the bugs across the water."

Max felt like kicking himself. The signs had been there all along. No wonder Reptile Island had seemed deserted. The lizards were all hiding, under the orders of General Komodo, waiting to ambush them. No wonder Spike had been so easy to find, with

only one guard – a fearsome one, true, but that must have been to make the trap more convincing.

"The bugs will never surrender to you," Barton said. "Even if all of us here are destroyed, new leaders will rise."

"Spare me the inspiring speeches," Komodo sneered. "Your bug forces might recover from the loss of Barton or his human adviser, but both?"

Nobody spoke as Komodo's words sank in. The trouble was, Komodo was right and they all knew it. The bugs would never recover from such a blow.

"So now what?" Max demanded.

Komodo looked up towards the volcano, and a strange look came into his golden eyes. "Now . . . I honour the volcano."

"What?" Max asked.

"Did you expect to be eaten? Oh, no. A far worse fate awaits you. Guards! Escort them to Great Reptilicus!"

The lizards began to march the bugs back up the side of the volcano. Max whispered to Barton, "What on earth is this 'Great Reptilicus' he's talking about?"

"I think he means the volcano," Barton whispered back.

Komodo overheard. "Mighty is the Great Reptilicus. His breath is fire! His blood is molten rock!"

The volcano rumbled. The lizards made sounds of awe.

Suddenly it was clear what Komodo meant

to do. In that dreadful moment Max wished he'd never picked up the *Encyclopedia* all those weeks ago.

"Barton, he's going to throw us into the volcano!"

Komodo's triumphant laugh told him he was right. "My reptile troops might want to eat you, human, but that is too good for you after all the trouble you've caused our forces."

None of the bugs spoke as the lizards herded them up the volcano. Max struggled to think of a way out of this. Try as he might, he couldn't. His mind felt like it was trapped in quicksand.

Then Max looked over his shoulder and saw what was coming up behind them, and his heart sank lower than ever.

All across the island, lizards were coming out of hiding, wriggling out of the sand, emerging from cracks in the rocks, and scampering out of caves and hollows. Iguanas, crested lizards, snakes, chameleons, turtles . . . dozens of them, then hundreds, then thousands. They covered the ground in a living carpet of creatures, all falling into step behind Komodo.

Every single reptile on Reptile Island was coming – slithering, crawling, hopping, and gliding – to watch Komodo's final victory.

As the procession reached the crater at the volcano's very top, Barton made a sudden bid for freedom. He launched himself into the air, whirring his great wings furiously.

"Go, Barton!" Max cheered.

But three gliding lizards leapt up and caught Barton at once. They pulled him to the ground. Barton struggled and fought, but more and more of the lizards piled on until he was pinned, unable to move at all.

The ground trembled beneath their feet. The bugs stood at the edge of the crater, looking down. Inside the volcano, boiling lava bubbled and spurted, sending gouts of glowing matter up into the air.

"End of the road," gloated one of the winged lizards.

RESCUE OPERATION

Max stood on the edge of the crater, hoping for a miracle. And then, as the last of his hope was dying, he heard a distant sound, coming closer, fast.

Buzz? No, it wasn't the high-pitched drone of the giant hornet's wings. It was a deeper, stronger sound . . . the noise of something *big*.

He looked towards Bug Island. A colossal black shape came thundering over the sea, zooming over the beach and up to the volcano. The crowd of watching lizards gasped.

Max grinned. Only one flying insect was *that* large.

"Dobs!" Max yelled happily and waved his arms. "Over here!"

Dobs heard him. The mighty insect swept down close, the wind from his wings flinging sand and dust everywhere, as if he was an approaching rescue helicopter. The gliding lizards backed away, trying to keep the sand out of their eyes.

Only Komodo stood his ground, but with sand flying into his mouth, he couldn't shout orders. "Mmmf!" he grunted. "Grrm blrgrh the buffle mmmgn!" Nobody could understand him.

Dobs hovered just above the ground. The windstorm from his wings blew up a cloud of dust so thick it hid the Battle Bugs from view. Max could hear the lizards yelling in anger.

"I THOUGHT YOU MIGHT NEED A LIFT," Dobs boomed.

"Yes please!" Max yelled back.

Once again, Dobs's huge pincers closed around him, gently lifting him off the ground.

"Grab my leg," Max yelled down to Webster. "We're getting out of here."

The timid spider wrapped himself

around Max's leg. "Ready!" he called.

"Now, Gigantus. Grab on to Webster!"

The centipede gripped tightly on to Webster's rear legs. Dobs beat his wings as hard as he could, taking the extra weight.

Barton was still struggling under a pile of lizards. "Get out," Barton cried. "Save yourselves."

"Not without you," Max said. He glanced down and saw that Spike was braced for action. "Spike, *now!*"

Spike slammed his stinger into the topmost lizard. The reptile roared in pain and released its grip. Another sting, and another, and another – and suddenly Barton burst free from the heap of groaning lizards.

"Payback time! That's for taking me prisoner, you big ugly newts!" Spike yelled.

"Spike, grab hold of Gigantus."

"Who's 'not important' now, eh?"

"Spike!"

"Oh, sorry!" Spike caught hold of Gigantus with both pincers.

"Dobs, GO!" Max yelled.

Dobs slowly rose up, straining as hard as he could. Above him hovered Barton, battered but alive. Below him dangled a living chain: Max, then Webster, then Gigantus, then Spike.

"Can he really lift all of us?" squeaked Webster.

"Only one way to find out!" Gigantus said.

Max held his breath as the airborne

group flew up and over the volcano's edge. Dobs bobbed unsteadily in the air and his wings thundered as if they were about to snap off, but Max knew he was going to make it. They flew back down the volcano slope, only just above the lizards. Max looked down at thousands of reptile faces watching them in anger.

"Careful, Dobs!" shouted Spike. "Gliding lizards incoming!"

The slender lizards came bounding down the mountainside, leaping up at the escaping bugs. With every leap they spread their arms and glided a short way, snapping as they went. One of them almost caught Spike. "Gliding lizards!" he roared. "I can't stand them!"

"Dobs, can you take evasive action?" Max asked.

"SORRY, MAX," Dobs said. "THEY'RE COMING AT ME FROM BEHIND. CAN'T DODGE THEM."

Max couldn't believe it. They'd come so close to escaping, only to be brought down at the last minute.

Dobs was nearly over the beach now, but the gliding lizards were keeping up, and coming closer with each attack. As if that wasn't enough, there was a dark cloud looming over them.

"Wait," Max said. "That's no cloud!"

The next second the sky was suddenly filled with screaming hornets, gleaming black and gold in the sunlight, diving down to attack the lizards.

"It's Buzz!" Webster yelled happily. "She brought reinforcements!"

"Not a moment too soon," added Barton.

As the hornets bombarded the gliding lizards with stings, Buzz flew up alongside them. "You're all clear, Max! Head on back to base. We'll keep the bogies off your back."

"Thanks, Buzz!"

"Excellent flying, Dobs," Buzz added. "You're a credit to the Battle Bugs. We're lucky to have you on our side." Then, in a flash, she was gone to join her fellow hornets.

Dobs didn't say anything, but Max was sure his wings were beating all the stronger now. He made it all the way across the sea to Bug Island before stopping for a rest. The grateful bugs climbed down on to the ground of their own island.

"Nice job, Dobs," said Spike. Webster and Gigantus agreed. The giant dobsonfly glowed with pride.

"I know I'm not much of a fighter bug," he admitted. "But I can carry a lot."

"You were just the right bug for the job," Max told him. "You saved our lives."

"Look at that. The 'Great Reptilicus' is angry," said Barton.

Over on Reptile Island, the volcano was belching out huge clouds of smoke. A ferocious blast of lava exploded into the sky and fell down like a fiery rain across the island. The lizards were probably cow-ering in fear.

"That's the best welcome-home present I could have asked for!" Spike said.

"Good to have you back, buddy," said Max with a grin. "Guess I'd better head home myself."

"Until next time, Max," Barton said. "Komodo will want revenge for this humili-ation. I have a feeling we will need your remarkable brain more than ever in the days to come."

Max held his magnifying glass up to the sky. Instantly, there was a sucking, whoosh-ing noise and he was whisked up into the air.

The next moment, he fell down into the human world, back into his school, between the library stacks . . . and landed right on top of a pushcart full of books. It toppled over with a CRASH.

"What was that?" cried Mrs Marquette from somewhere off in the distance. "Don't move. I'm coming!"

Uh-oh, Max thought to himself, and began to sneak towards the exit. *Time for another stealthy escape . . .*

REAL LIFE
BATTLE BUGS!

Giant Centipede

Found across the continent of South America and on the islands of the Caribbean, the giant centipede is one of the largest representatives of its genus in the world. It can easily reach ten inches in length, and some have even been known to grow up to an enormous twelve inches.

The giant centipede is one aggressive arthropod. It feeds on a whole variety of vertebrates and invertebrates, including frogs, lizards and birds. If it comes across something it is able to catch and kill, it will happily devour it.

The giant centipede is a clever critter, too. It has been known to dangle upside down from the roofs of caves in order to catch passing bats. Grabbing on to the unsuspecting creatures with its many legs, the centipede then injects venom into its victim using sharp claws called forcipules. The venom contains chemicals that are fatal to small animals. Even in humans, the poison can cause severe pain and fever.

All in all, the giant centipede is a bug

that is not to be messed with!

Trapdoor Spider

Trapdoor spiders get their name from the way they catch their prey. After using their fangs and forelegs to burrow down into the ground, they fashion a "trapdoor" made of vegetation, soil and their own silk. Then, they lie in wait just under the door, until an unsuspecting victim trips the silk wire outside the burrow, and the spider strikes.

However, this formidable predator doesn't always find itself with the upper hand; sometimes it, too, comes under attack. If a spider wasp spots a trapdoor spider, it will attack it until the arachnid is forced to retreat. But even when the spider thinks it's safe in its hole, the wasp can destroy the trapdoor with its fangs and sting the spider. Then, the wasp lays its eggs on the trapdoor spider, so that when the larvae hatch, they have an eight-legged meal for the taking!

Dobsonfly

The dobsonfly is a large insect distributed throughout the Americas, Asia and South Africa. It inhabits aquatic areas, and is particularly common around streams, swamps and other waterways. Apart from butterflies, dobsonflies are some of the largest insects in the world. Their wingspans can reach up to seven inches, and vary in colour from grey to translucent.

These insects are generalist predators, which means that they feed on a wide variety of things. As nocturnal insects, they emerge at night to ambush their prey, which is mostly made up of young mayflies, midges and other small flying insects.

THE ADVENTURE CONTINUES!

The time has come for the Battle Bugs to drive General Komodo's reptilian forces off Bug Island once and for all. Using all the knowledge Max has gained in his time with the Battle Bugs, he must lead the bug army in an all-out attack. If they don't defeat the lizard army this time, Bug Island will be lost – for ever.

Make sure you ask an adult to cut out the bug for you. The bug should be cut along the solid black lines. The dotted lines are for folding.

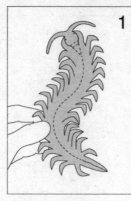

1

Start by cutting out your bug. It should look like this.

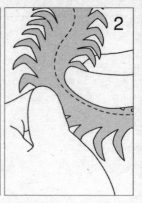

2

Fold the dotted lines running along the spine of the bug.

3

Form the triangle fold below the head. Then fold the base of the head into the step fold shown above. Next fold the two antennas at the top of the head back on themselves along the dotted lines.

4

Fold the two dotted lines at the base of the spine backwards to make the tail.

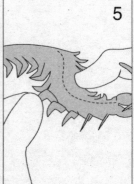

5

Finally, fold the dotted lines on each leg.